Civil Rights

by Martha London

Consultant: Emma Ryan, Social Studies Educator

BEARPORT
PUBLISHING

Minneapolis, Minnesota

Credits

Cover, © Orphan Cam/Shutterstock; Title page, © Lightspring/Shutterstock; 5 © AnnGaysorn/ Shutterstock; 7, © kali9/iStock; 8, © Everett Collection/Shutterstock; 9, © Jack R Perry Photography/ Shutterstock; 11, © AP/Shutterstock; 13, © Everett Collection Historical/Alamy; 14, © Nigel Jarvis/ Shutterstock; 15, © Everett Collection/Shutterstock; 17, © Icom Images/Alamy; 19, © Science History Image s/Alamy; 21, © Homer Sykes/Alamy; 23T, © garetsworkshop/Shutterstock; 23B, © Twinsterphoto/ Shutterstock; 25T, © Neil Atkinson; 25C, © CHOONGKY/Shutterstock; 25B, © Pacific Press Media Production Corp./Alamy; 27, © ASDF_MEDIA/Shutterstock; 28T, © WDC Photos/Alamy; 28C, © Araya Doheny/Getty Images; and 28B, © GIORGIO VIERA/EFE/Newscom.

Bearport Publishing Company Product Development Team

President: Jen Jenson; Director of Product Development: Spencer Brinker; Senior Editor: Allison Juda; Editor: Charly Haley; Associate Editor: Naomi Reich; Senior Designer: Colin O'Dea; Associate Designer: Elena Klinkner; Product Development Assistant: Anita Stasson

Quote Sources

Page 28: Anthony Kennedy from "Supreme Court Rules In Favor of Marriage Equality," *MSNBC*, June 17, 2015; Tatiana Lee from "30 Years Later: How The ADA Changed Life For People With Disabilities," *Forbes*, July 21, 2020; Alicia Garza from "Interview With #BlackLivesMatter Co-Founder Alicia Garza," *Forbes*, Jan. 15, 2021.

Library of Congress Cataloging-in-Publication Data is available at www.loc.gov or upon request from the publisher.

ISBN: 978-0-7166-4946-5 (hardcover)

This edition is co-published by agreement between Bearport Publishing and World Book, Inc.

Bearport Publishing
5357 Penn Avenue South
Minneapolis, MN 55419
www.bearportpublishing.com

World Book, Inc.
180 North LaSalle Street, Suite 900
Chicago, IL 60601
www.worldbook.com

Contents

Access for Everyone

Thousands of students in the United States use wheelchairs. School buildings must have wheelchair ramps for them. Why? A law tells schools and other public places to give equal **access** to everyone. This kind of law protects people's civil rights.

The American Disabilities Act (ADA) became a law in 1990. This law makes sure people with disabilities have equal rights. It covers everything from requiring ramps to allowing service animals in public places.

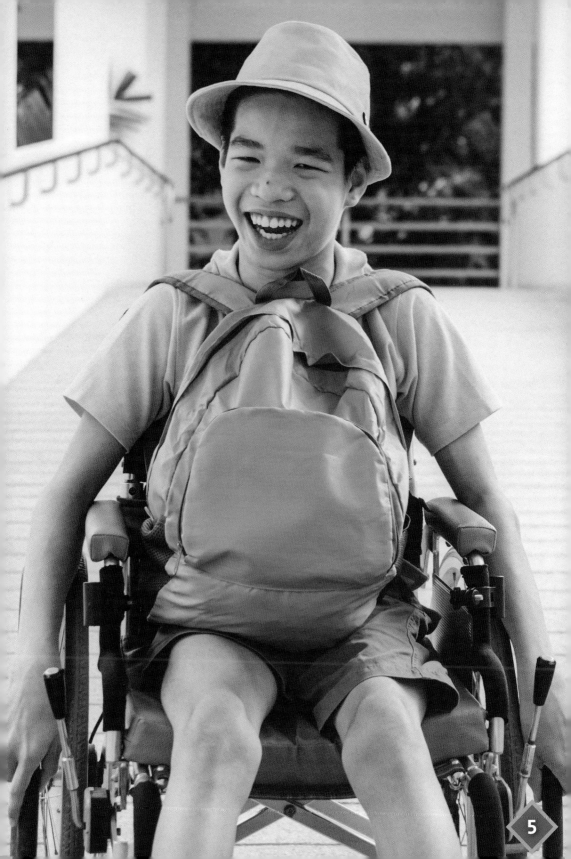

What Are Civil Rights?

Civil rights make sure people have equal treatment by law. The laws protect people from **discrimination**. They say a person cannot be treated differently because of their race, gender, religion, or other traits including disabilities.

There are many kinds of civil rights. One example is the right to vote. Another is the right to be treated fairly at work or school.

A Bold Beginning

Civil rights were not always a part of U.S. laws. The first ones came after the Civil War (1861–1865). They were in the 13th, 14th, and 15th amendments. These changes to the Constitution banned slavery. The laws made Black people citizens. They also gave Black men the right to vote.

In 1920, the 19th Amendment gave women the right to vote. This change came after years of women protesting to be treated fairly.

The U.S. Constitution

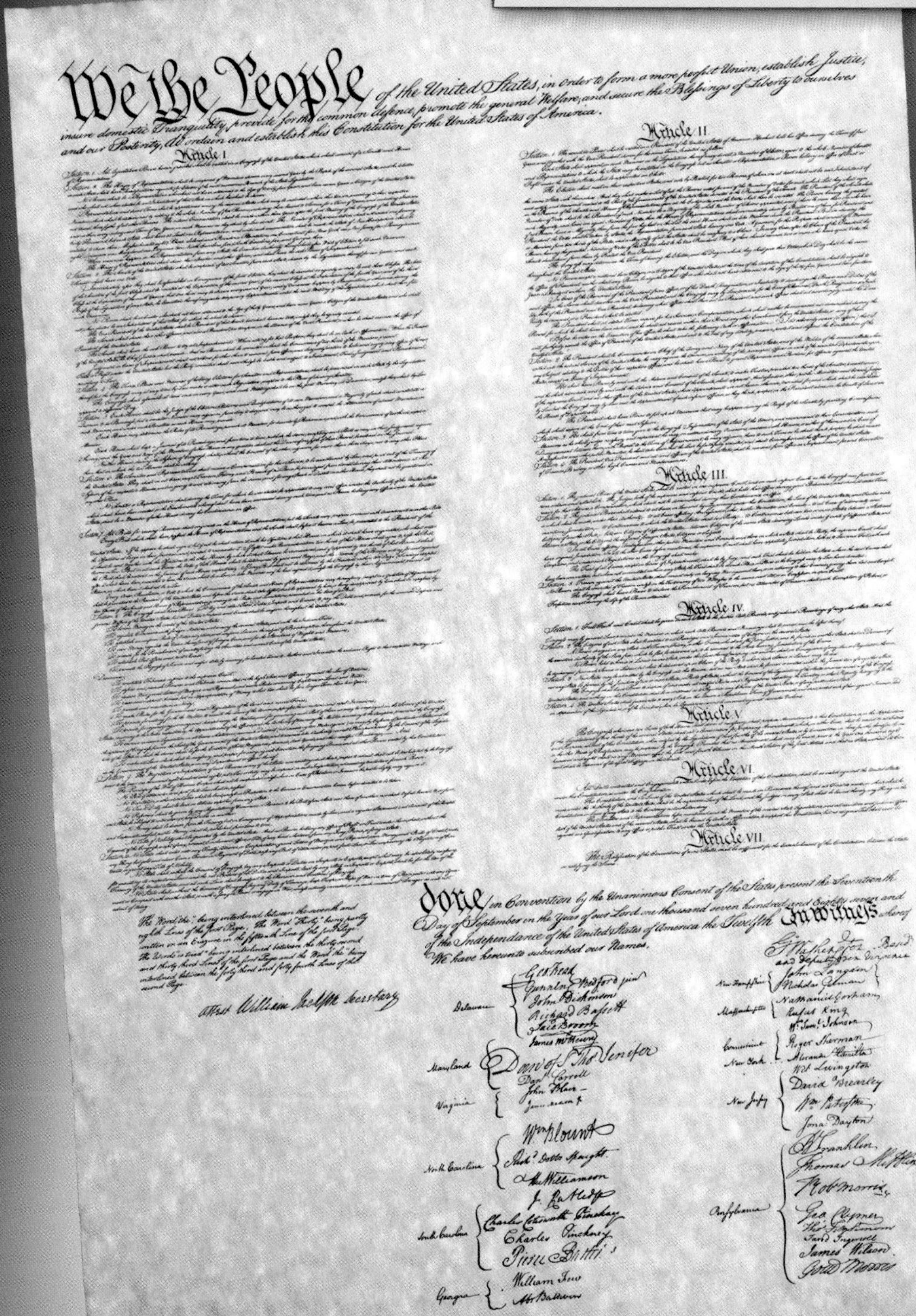
We the People of the United States, in Order to form a more perfect Union, establish Justice, insure domestic Tranquility, provide for the common defence, promote the general Welfare, and secure the Blessings of Liberty to ourselves and our Posterity, do ordain and establish this Constitution for the United States of America.

Article I

Article II

Article III

Article IV

Article V

Article VI

Article VII

done in Convention by the Unanimous Consent of the States present the Seventeenth Day of September in the Year of our Lord one thousand seven hundred and Eighty seven and of the Independance of the United States of America the Twelfth In witness whereof We have hereunto subscribed our Names.

Even with these amendments, Black people faced a lot of discrimination. They were often harmed. Some other laws from the early 1900s made things worse. Black people were forced to separate from White people in public places. This was called **segregation**.

Segregation let different groups be treated differently. Black-only schools did not get as much money as White schools. Black people were not allowed to live in certain places. Good jobs were given only to White people.

A Movement Like No Other

Segregation continued for years, even though it was very unfair. Then, in the 1950s and 1960s, many people began protesting. They wanted more laws to protect Black people. This fight for change became known as the civil rights movement.

People protested in many ways. Sometimes, they went to segregated places and wouldn't leave. Other times, thousands of people marched together.

Peaceful **activists** in the movement often faced violence. They were attacked by people who wanted to keep segregation. But the protesters did not give up.

On August 28, 1963, more than 200,000 people met in Washington, D.C. They asked for better laws.

On this August day, Dr. Martin Luther King Jr. gave his famous "I Have a Dream" speech. King is one of the most well-known civil rights leaders in history.

This event became known as the March on Washington.

New Laws

A year later, the Civil Rights Act of 1964 passed. This law stopped segregation. It also banned other forms of discrimination at work and school. The law was a huge victory for Black activists. But it helped other groups, too. Later civil rights laws followed the example of the Civil Rights Act.

Part of the Civil Rights Act said all people must be treated fairly at job interviews. The law also said people cannot be fired from jobs because of their race, gender, or religion.

President Johnson signed the Civil Rights Act into law.

The Indian Civil Rights Act of 1968 gave Native Americans citizen rights for the first time. In the 1800s, Native Americans had been forced onto **reservations**. These lands had their own laws. But the Indian Civil Rights Act said people living there must be treated fairly by U.S. laws, too.

Another important civil rights law was the Fair Housing Act of 1968. This said all people should be treated fairly while renting or buying a home.

President Calvin Coolidge meets with Native Americans

Another Fight for Rights

While the civil rights movement was happening, women also protested for more rights. They had won the right to vote in 1920. But women also wanted to be paid the same as men in similar jobs. Their protests led to the Equal Pay Act of 1963.

Since the 1920s, women have fought for the Equal Rights Amendment (ERA). This would ban all discrimination based on gender.

Winning in Court

New laws are not the only way to make important changes. Civil rights wins have also happened in courtrooms. For many years, people of the same gender could not get married. **LGBTQ** activists fought to change this. In 2015, the Supreme Court said gay people could be legally married.

The Supreme Court based its decision on laws that were already in place. The judges said the Constitution already let people get married without discrimination.

Modern Movements

Today, many groups are still protesting. Black Lives Matter activists work to stop police violence against Black people. Stop Asian Hate protesters want safety for Asian Americans. And the #MeToo movement fights against sexual harassment. People hope these efforts will lead to a better future.

The #MeToo movement started online in 2017. Women, LGBTQ people, and others shared stories about being sexually harassed. The stories brought attention to this big problem.

Moving Forward

Many people have had important victories in gaining civil rights. But there is more work to do. Over time, people may face new kinds of discrimination. Activists may need to find new ways to fight for better laws. This way, everyone will be protected by civil rights.

Some people face more than one form of discrimination. A Black woman might be treated unfairly based on her gender and her race. A gay person who uses a wheelchair may face discrimination in many ways, too.

By working together, people can change laws to help everyone.

Voices
in the News

People have many things to say about civil rights. Some of their voices can be heard in the news.

Anthony Kennedy
Supreme Court Justice

"[LGBTQ people] ask for [equality] in the eyes of the law. The Constitution grants them that right."

Tatiana Lee
Disability activist

"Most of the time, being a person with a disability, the disability is not the hard part. The hard part is people's attitudes toward your disability."

Alicia Garza
Black Lives Matter co-founder

"You have to believe that change can happen if you are going to be a part of making change."

★ SilverTips for REVIEW

Review what you've learned. Use the text to help you.

Define key terms

activist

amendment

civil rights

discrimination

protest

Check for understanding

What are civil rights? Give one example.

Describe how civil rights have changed over time.

What work have people done to change laws and gain civil rights?

Think deeper

What are some of the civil rights you have because of movements of the past? Are there any ongoing challenges to your rights?

★ SilverTips on TEST-TAKING

- **Make a study plan.** Ask your teacher what the test is going to cover. Then, set aside time to study a little bit every day.

- **Read all the questions carefully.** Be sure you know what is being asked.

- **Skip any questions** you don't know how to answer right away. Mark them and come back later if you have time.

Glossary

access the ability to go somewhere or use something

activists people working toward change

amendments official changes made to the U.S. Constitution

citizens people who are from and of a country

constitution the system of laws for a country, state, or organization

discrimination purposeful mistreatment of a person or group because of a trait

LGBTQ an abbreviation for lesbian, gay, bisexual, transgender, and queer, which represents people from a variety of genders and sexual orientations

protesting taking action showing disagreement with laws or society

reservations areas of land set aside by the U.S. government for Native Americans

segregation a forced separation of people by race

sexual harassment unwanted touches or comments from another person

Read More

Loh-Hagan, Virginia. *LGBTQ+ Rights (Stand Up, Speak Out).* Ann Arbor, MI: Cherry Lake Publishing, 2021.

Markovics, Joyce. *2020 Black Lives Matter Marches (Protest! March for Change).* Ann Arbor, MI: Cherry Lake Publishing, 2021.

Wilkins, Veronica B. *Civil Rights Movement (Turning Points in U.S. History).* Minneapolis: Jump!, 2020.

Learn More Online

1. Go to **www.factsurfer.com** or scan the QR code below.

2. Enter "**Civil Rights**" into the search box.

3. Click on the cover of this book to see a list of websites.

Index

About the Author

Martha London is a writer and educator in Minnesota. She lives with her cat.